Hey Jack! Books

First American Edition 2021
Kane Miller, A Division of EDC Publishing
Original Title: Hey Jack: The Other Teacher
Text Copyright © 2014 Sally Rippin
Illustration Copyright © 2014 Stephanie Spartels
Logo and Design Copyright © 2014 Hardie Grant Children's Publishing
First published in Australia by Hardie Grant Children's Publishing

For information contact:
Kane Miller, A Division of EDC Publishing
5402 S 122nd E Ave, Tulsa, OK 74146
www.kanemiller.com
www.myubam.com
Library of Congress Control Number: 2021934583
Printed and bound in the United States of America
1 2 3 4 5 6 7 8 9 10
ISBN: 978-1-68464-307-3

The Other Teacher

By Sally Rippin

Illustrated by Stephanie Spartels

Kane Miller
A DIVISION OF EDC PUBLISHING

Worried face

Jittery tummy

Legs that don't want to walk to school

Anxious Mood

Chapter One

This is Jack. Today Jack
is in an anxious mood.
His teacher, Ms. Walton,
is going away for a
whole term!

Jack loves Ms. Walton.
She is a great teacher.
He is very **worried** that
the new teacher won't
be as nice as Ms. Walton.

Jack and Billie walk
to school together.
Billie skips along the
sidewalk. Jack drags
his feet.

"I'm excited to meet our new teacher," says Billie. "Are you excited, Jack?"

"I guess so," says Jack. But he feels his tummy squeeze as tight as a ball.

What if she is too bossy? Jack worries. *Or, even worse, what if she is not bossy enough?*

Jack and Billie arrive at their classroom. The new teacher is already there. She has written her name on the board.

Miss Anna Capaldi

"Hello, everyone!" she calls in a bright voice.

Everyone in the classroom **wriggles** with excitement. They all look at each other, grinning.

"My name is Miss Capaldi," she says. "But you can call me Anna."

Jack gasps. *Anna? That doesn't sound like a teacher's name!*

The new teacher continues, "I thought we might change the classroom around. It would be good to try something new. Does anyone have any suggestions?"

Rebecca shoots up her hand. "What about we put the desks in a circle?" she says.

That won't work, thinks Jack. *Half the class won't be able to see the board!*

"I like that idea," the new teacher smiles. "Any other suggestions?"

Sam puts up his hand. "What about if we work in groups? We can move the desks together to be with our friends."

"That's a good idea, too," the teacher says.

Jack feels funny. His tummy gets tighter and tighter.

Oh dear, he thinks. *Sam and Benny will never get their work done if they sit together. Ms. Walton always has to separate them!*

Then Miss Anna Capaldi smiles.

"I've had an even better idea," she says in her bright singsong voice.

"It's a glorious day outside. Why don't we go out and sit on the playground?"

Everyone in the class cheers **excitedly**.

Jack can't help feeling excited too. Going outside sounds like a lot of fun. But he still feels very worried.

What if the new teacher forgets to teach them anything?

Chapter Two

The kids in Jack's classroom run out onto the playground. They squeal and shout and laugh.

Benny and Sam race
each other to the far end
of the field. Rebecca and
Lola start a cartwheel
competition on the grass.

Oh dear, Jack worries. *The new teacher will be so angry!*

Just then Billie taps him on the shoulder. "You're it!" she shouts. Jack forgets his worries and chases after Billie.

"All right, everyone!" Anna calls. "Come and sit down in front of me."

Jack stops running.
But nobody else listens.
Benny and Sam are too
far away. Rebecca and
Lola are too busy doing
cartwheels. Even Billie
is still running around.

Jack bites his fingernails.
It makes him **anxious**
to see everyone ignoring
their new teacher.

Just then, Anna does a strange thing. She sits down on the grass and begins to sing a song. Not in a loud voice. Just a quiet voice.

One by one, the kids stop laughing and shouting. They sit down on the grass beside Anna to listen. It is a strange song about numbers. Jack sits down, too.

"One two is two and two twos are four. Three twos are six and four twos are eight …" she sings.

Rebecca and Lola stop cartwheeling. Sam and Benny run back to sit down, too. Soon everyone is listening to the new teacher sing.

"OK, now it's your turn," Anna says, smiling. To Jack's amazement, everyone tries to sing along as best as they can.

It's the two times table!
Jack realizes.

They do the five times table. Then the ten.

Sometimes Anna adds in a funny mistake to check that everyone is paying attention. They always laugh.

Benny and Sam roll around on the grass laughing. Rebecca and Lola sometimes do cartwheels, but they still sing.

They are halfway through the eleven times table when the bell goes. Everyone runs back to class to get their snack for recess.

"Wasn't that fun?" Billie says, running alongside Jack.

"Definitely," says Jack.

But they are not really
doing any schoolwork.
They have just been
playing games.

After recess, Anna tells
them they are going to
do science.

Jack feels relieved.
He pulls his workbook
out of his desk and begins
to sharpen his pencils.

Jack loves science.
Now, at least they
will be doing some
real work!

"No need for books!"
Anna smiles. "We are
going to do field work
outside."

Field work? Jack wonders
what that is, and
whether it will be hard.

The class runs outside ahead of Anna.

The new teacher strides out into the middle of the field. She doesn't even bother calling all the students that have spread far and wide. She just begins to sing again. This time it is a song about a caterpillar.

The caterpillar eats leaves and spins itself a cocoon. Then it turns into a butterfly.

All the kids gather around to hear Anna's song. She teaches them the words.

Then she teaches them another song about the life cycle of a frog.

They learn another
one about the seasons.
And another one about
evaporation.

"How do you know all
these songs?" Billie asks.

Anna shrugs. "I just make
them up as I go along,"
she says. "I have a terrible
memory. I have to turn
everything into a song."

Anna laughs. "It's the only way I can remember things. I even sing my phone number!" She sings it for them.

Everyone laughs and tries singing their own phone numbers.

Just then, the bell goes. Jack can't believe how quickly the day is passing.

And they haven't even
sat down to do any real
work yet!

Chapter Three

After lunch, the new
teacher tells the class
they will stay inside.
She asks them to take
out their workbooks.

Finally, we are doing some real work! thinks Jack.

"I want you to write down everything you have learned today," Anna says.

Jack opens his workbook to a new page. He takes out his sharpest pencil. He is not sure they have learned anything today!

But then, he thinks
about the times tables.
The twos, fives, and tens.
He can never usually
remember how they go.
He begins to hum.

One two is two, two twos are four … Before he even realizes what is happening, he has written the whole two times table down.

He tries again with the five times table. *One five is five, two fives are ten* … Once again, he remembers all of them.

It's the same with the
tens. Soon his whole
page is covered with
times tables.

Jack is surprised how easily he remembers them all.

He looks up. All his classmates have their heads bent over their workbooks. He has never seen Sam and Benny concentrating so hard. Rebecca and Lola are concentrating too.

Everyone is humming quietly to themselves. Jack giggles. It sounds a little like being in a classroom of bees!

He looks to the front of the classroom. Anna is sitting at her desk. She looks up at Jack and smiles. Jack smiles back.

Having a new teacher isn't so bad after all, he thinks. He still misses Ms. Walton. Anna is totally different from her.

But maybe Anna can teach us other things in this funny way she has?

Jack opens up a new page of his workbook.

He begins to write
down the life cycle of
the caterpillar.

And before he can stop himself, Jack is humming another song.